DISCARD

P9-DNM-924

Chicago Public Library

Chicago, IL 60631

THE PETER YARROW SONGBOOK

Favorite Folk Songs

ILLUSTRATED BY

Terry Widener

STERLING

New York / London

I dedicate this book to Charlie Nurnberg and Frances Gilbert who conceived of this project,
brought it to life, and made it into something of which I am extraordinarily proud.

I dedicate my performances on the accompanying CD with everlasting
gratitude and love to Mary Travers and Noel Paul Stookey. —P. Y.

To my children, and my wife, Leslie, who sang them lullabies.
And to my French agent, Michele. —T. M. W.

STERLING and the distinctive Sterling logo are registered trademarks of Sterling Publishing Co., Inc.

Library of Congress Cataloging-in-Publication Data Available

2 4 6 8 10 9 7 5 3

Published by Sterling Publishing Co., Inc.
387 Park Avenue South, New York, NY 10016
All songs are traditional with new lyrics and music by Peter Yarrow and Bethany Yarrow © 2008
Silver Dawn Music, ASCAP
Additional text © 2008 by Peter Yarrow
Illustrations © 2008 by Terry Widener
Distributed in Canada by Sterling Publishing
c/o Canadian Manda Group, 165 Dufferin Street
Toronto, Ontario, Canada M6K 3H6
Distributed in the United Kingdom by GMC Distribution Services Castle Place,
166 High Street, Lewes, East Sussex, England BN7 1XU
Distributed in Australia by Capricorn Link (Australia) Pty. Ltd.
P.O. Box 704, Windsor, NSW 2756, Australia

Printed in China
All rights reserved

Sterling ISBN 978-1-4027-5961-1

For information about custom editions, special sales,
premium and corporate purchases, please contact
Sterling Special Sales Department at 800-805-5489
or specialsales@sterlingpublishing.com.

The artwork for this book was created using acrylic paints.

Designed by Judythe Sieck and Scott Piehl.

R042662246

CHICAGO PUBLIC LIBRARY
RODEN BRANCH
6083 NORTHWEST HGWY. 60631

CONTENTS

INTRODUCTION
PETER YARROW

In recording some of my favorite folk songs for this collection, I was struck by how much I still loved them and how much they had taught me about life. Folk songs were written for the simple necessity of telling the news—the joys and the sorrows—of people like us who lived long ago. Singing these songs today allows us to experience the history and spirit of times past and also makes us feel closer to one another.

Please think of these songs as more than performances, though I hope you will find them entertaining and moving. You might start out by singing along with my daughter, Bethany, and me. But later I hope you will sing them on your own, with your friends and family, accompanied by a few guitar chords or even a capella.

These songs have inspired me and helped to give me a sense of purpose in my life.
I hope that your life will be similarly inspired.

The Golden Vanity

There was a ship that sailed all on the lowland sea,
And the name of the ship was the *Golden Vanity*.
And we feared she would be taken by the Spanish enemy
As she sailed upon the lowland, lowland, lowland,
Sailed upon the lowland sea.

Then up spoke the cabin boy, and boldly out spoke he,
And he said to our captain, "What will you give to me,
If I swim along the side of the Spanish enemy
And I sink her in the lowland, lowland, lowland,
Sink her in the lowland sea?"

"Oh, I will give you silver, and I will give you gold,
And my own fair young daughter, your bonny bright shall be,
If you'll swim along the side of the Spanish enemy
And you sink her in the lowland, lowland, lowland,
Sink her in the lowland sea.

Then the boy made him ready, and overboard sprang he,
And he swam along the side of the Spanish enemy.
With his brace and auger in her side he bored holes three,
And he sank her in the lowland, lowland, lowland,
Sank her in the lowland sea.

Then quickly he swam back to the cheering of the crew,
But the captain would not heed him, his promise he did rue.
And he scorned his poor entreatings when loudly he did sue,
And he left him in the lowland, lowland, lowland,
Left him in the lowland sea.

Then his messmates drew him up, but on the deck he died.
And they stitched him in a hammock which was so fair and white.
Then they lowered him overboard, and he drifted with the tide,
And he sank into the lowland, lowland, lowland,
Sank into the lowland sea.

There was a ship that sailed all on the lowland sea,
And the name of the ship was the *Golden Vanity*.
And we feared she would be taken by the Spanish enemy
As she sailed upon the lowland, lowland, lowland,
Sailed upon the lowland sea.

As she sailed upon the lowland, lowland, lowland,
Sailed upon the lowland sea.

Skip to My Lou

Skip, skip, skip to my Lou,
Skip, skip, skip to my Lou,
Skip, skip, skip to my Lou,
Skip to my Lou, my darlin'.

Lost my partner, what'll I do?
Lost my partner, what'll I do?
Lost my partner, what'll I do?
Skip to my Lou, my darlin'.

Skip, skip, skip to my Lou,
Skip, skip, skip to my Lou,
Skip, skip, skip to my Lou,
Skip to my Lou, my darlin'.

I'll get another one, prettier than you,
I'll get another one, nicer than you,
I'll get another one, nicer than you,
Skip to my Lou, my darlin'.

Skip, skip, skip to my Lou,
Skip, skip, skip to my Lou,
Skip, skip, skip to my Lou,
Skip to my Lou, my darlin'.

Fly's in the buttermilk, shoo, fly, shoo,
Fly's in the buttermilk, shoo, fly, shoo,
Fly's in the buttermilk, shoo, fly, shoo,
Skip to my Lou, my darlin'.

Skip, skip, skip to my Lou,
Skip, skip, skip to my Lou,
Skip, skip, skip to my Lou,
Skip to my Lou, my darlin'.

Little red wagon painted blue,
Little red wagon painted blue,
Little red wagon painted blue,
Skip to my Lou, my darlin'.

Skip, skip, skip to my Lou,
Skip, skip, skip to my Lou,
Skip, skip, skip to my Lou,
Skip to my Lou, my darlin'.

Cockles and Mussels

In Dublin's fair city, where girls are so pretty,
There I first laid my eyes on sweet Molly Malone,
As she wheeled her wheelbarrow
Through the streets broad and narrow,
Crying, "Cockles and mussels, alive, alive-o!"

"Alive, alive-o-oh! Alive, alive-o-oh!"
Crying, "Cockles and mussels, alive, alive-o!"

She was a fishmonger, and sure 'twas no wonder,
'Cause her mother and father were fishmongers too.
And they all wheeled their barrow
Through the streets broad and narrow,
Crying, "Cockles and mussels, alive, alive-o!"

"Alive, alive-o-oh! Alive, alive-o-oh!"
Crying, "Cockles and mussels, alive, alive-o!"

She died of the fever, and no one could save her,
And that was the end of sweet Molly Malone.
Now her ghost wheels the barrow
Through the streets broad and narrow,
Crying, "Cockles and mussels, alive, alive-o!"

"Alive, alive-o-oh! Alive, alive-o-oh!"
Crying, "Cockles and mussels, alive, alive-o!"

The Fox

Oh, the fox went out on a chilly night,
Prayed for the moon to give him light,
For he had many a mile to go that night
Before he reached the town-o, town-o, town-o.
Many a mile to go that night before he
   reached the town-o.

He ran till he came to a great big pen
Where the ducks and the geese were kept therein.
He said, "A couple of you are gonna grease my chin
Before I leave this town-o, town-o, town-o.
A couple of you are gonna grease my chin before
   I leave this town-o!"

He grabbed the gray goose by the neck,
Flung him up across his back.
He didn't mind the "quack, quack, quack"
And the legs all danglin' down-o,
   down-o, down-o.
He didn't mind the "quack, quack, quack" and the legs
   all danglin' down-o.

Then old mother Flipper Flopper jumped out of bed,
Out of the window she popped her head,
Cryin', "John, John, the gray goose is gone
And the fox is on the town-o, town-o, town-o.
John! John! The gray goose is gone and the fox
    is on the town-o!"

Then John, he ran to the top of the hill,
Blew his horn both loud and shrill.
The fox, he said, "I better flee with my kill,
For they'll soon be on my trail-o, trail-o, trail-o."
The fox, he said, "I better flee with my kill, for they'll
    soon be on my trail-o!"

He ran till he came to his cozy den,
There were the little ones, eight, nine, ten.
They said, "Daddy, daddy, better go back again
'Cause it must be a mighty fine town-o, town-o,
    town-o.
Daddy, daddy, better go back again 'cause it
    must be a mighty fine town-o!"

Then the fox and his wife, without any strife,
Cut up the goose with a carving knife.
They never had such a supper in their life,
And the little ones chewed on the bones-o,
    bones-o, bones-o.
They never had such a supper in their life,
    and the little ones chewed on the bones-o!

The fox went out on a chilly night,
Prayed for the moon to give him light,
He had many a mile to go that night
Before he reached the town-o, town-o, town-o.
Many a mile to go that night before he
    reached the town-o.

Springfield Mountain

On Springfield Mountain there did dwell
A lovely youth, I knowed him well-aye-el.
Too roody noo, too roody nay,
Too roody noo, too roody nay-aye-ay.

This lovely youth one day did go
Down to the meadow for to mow-aye-oh.
Too roody noo, too roody nay,
Too roody noo, too roody nay-aye-ay.

He had not mowed quite round the field,
When a poison serpent bit his heel-aye-eel.
Too roody noo, too roody nay,
Too roody noo, too roody nay-aye-ay.

They took him home to Molly dear,
Which made him feel so very queer-aye-eer.
Too roody noo, too roody nay,
Too roody noo, too roody nay-aye-ay.

Now Molly had two ruby lips,
With which the poison she did sip-aye-ip.
Too roody noo, too roody nay,
Too roody noo, too roody nay-aye-ay.

Now Molly had a rotten tooth,
And so the poison killed them booth-aye-ooth.
Too roody noo, too roody nay,
Too roody noo, too roody nay-aye-ay.

On Springfield Mountain there did dwell
A lovely youth, I knowed him well-aye-el.
Too roody noo, too roody nay,
Too roody noo, too roody nay.

The Erie Canal

I've got a mule, her name is Sal,
Fifteen miles on the Erie Canal.
She's a good old worker and a good old pal,
Fifteen miles on the Erie Canal.

We've loaded barges in our day
Filled with lumber, coal, and hay.
And we know every inch of the way
From Albany to Buffalo.

Low bridge, everybody down!
Low bridge, 'cause we're comin' into town!
And you'll always know your neighbor,
You'll always know your pal,
If you've ever navigated the Erie Canal.

We'd better look around for a job, old gal,
Fifteen miles on the Erie Canal.
'Cause you bet your life I'd never part with Sal,
Fifteen miles on the Erie Canal.

Get up there mule, here comes a lock.
We'll make Rome 'bout six o'clock.
And one more trip and back we'll go
Right back home to Buffalo.

Low bridge, everybody down!
Low bridge, 'cause we're comin' into town!
And you'll always know your neighbor,
You'll always know your pal,
If we ever navigated on the Erie Canal.

Beautiful City

O, what a beautiful city,
O, what a beautiful city,
God knows, it's a beautiful city,
Twelve gates to the city, hallelujah.

Three gates to the north,
Three gates to the south,
Three gates to the east,
Three gates to the west.
There's twelve gates to the city, hallelujah.

O, what a beautiful city,
O, what a beautiful city,
God knows, it's a beautiful city,
Twelve gates to the city, hallelujah.

City of justice,
City of peace,
City of my own heart's release.

O, what a beautiful city,
O, what a beautiful city,
God knows, it's a beautiful city,
Twelve gates to the city, hallelujah.

19

Rock-a My Soul

Rock my soul in the bosom of Abraham,
Rock my soul in the bosom of Abraham,
Rock my soul in the bosom of Abraham,
O, rock-a my soul!

So high I can't get over it,
So low I can't get under it,
So wide I can't get round it,
O, rock-a my soul!

Rock my soul,
Rock my soul,
Rock my soul,
Rock my soul.

Rock my soul in the bosom of Abraham,
Rock my soul in the bosom of Abraham,
Rock my soul in the bosom of Abraham,
O, rock-a my soul!

The Cruel War

The cruel war is raging, and Johnny has to fight.
I want to be with him from morning till night.
I want to be with him, it grieves my heart so.
Won't you let me go with you?
No, my love, no.

Tomorrow is Sunday, and Monday is the day
That your captain will call you and you must obey.
Your captain will call you, it grieves my heart so.
Won't you let me go with you?
No, my love, no.

I'll tie back my hair, men's clothing I'll put on.
I'll pass as your comrade as we march along.
I'll pass as your comrade. No one will ever know.
Won't you let me go with you?
No, my love, no.

Your cheek is too ruddy, your fingers are too small,
Your skin still too fair to face the cannonball.
Won't you let me go with you? It grieves my heart so.
Won't you let me go with you?
No, my love, no.

Oh, Johnny, oh, Johnny, I fear you are unkind.
I love you far better than even my own life.
I love you far better than words can e'er express.
Won't you let me go with you?
Yes, my love, yes.

The cruel war is raging, and Johnny has to fight.
I want to be with him from morning till night.

O, Mary,
Don't You Weep

O, Mary, don't you weep, don't you mourn,
O, Mary, don't you weep, don't you mourn.
Pharaoh's army got drownded,
O, Mary, don't you weep.

If I could I surely would
Stand on the rock where Moses stood.
Pharaoh's army got drownded,
O, Mary, don't you weep.

O, Mary!

O, Mary, don't you weep, don't you mourn,
O, Mary, don't you weep, don't you mourn.
Pharaoh's army got drownded,
O, Mary, don't you weep.

One of these mornings 'bout twelve o'clock,
This whole world's gonna reel and rock.
Pharaoh's army got drownded,
O, Mary, don't you weep.

O, Mary!

O, Mary, don't you weep, don't you mourn,
O, Mary, don't you weep, don't you mourn.
Pharaoh's army got drownded,
O, Mary, don't you weep.

One of these mornings, and it won't be long,
We're gonna sing that freedom song.
Pharaoh's army got drownded,
O, Mary, don't you weep.

O, Mary!

O, Mary, don't you weep, don't you mourn,
O, Mary, don't you weep, don't you mourn.
Pharaoh's army got drownded,
O, Mary, don't you weep.

I've Been Workin' on the Railroad

I've been workin' on the railroad
All the live long day.
I've been workin' on the railroad
Just to pass the time away.
Can't ya hear the whistle blowing
Rise up so early in the morn.
Can't you hear the captain shouting,
"Dinah, blow your horn!"

Dinah, won't you blow,
Dinah, won't you blow,
Dinah, won't you blow your horn, your horn?
Dinah, won't you blow,
Dinah, won't you blow,
Dinah, won't you blow your horn?

Someone's in the kitchen with Dinah.
Someone's in the kitchen, I know.
Someone's in the kitchen with Dinah,
Strummin' on the old banjo, and singin'

"Fee, fie, fiddle-y-i-o,
Fee, fie, fiddle-y-i-o-o-o-o.
Fee, fie, fiddle-y-i-o."
Strummin' on the old banjo.

Sloop John B

We sail on the sloop John B,
My grandfather and me.
'Round Nassau town we did go.
Drinking all night,
Got into a fight.
I feel so broke up,
I want to go home.

So hoist up the John B sails,
See how the mainsail set.
Call for the captain ashore, let me go home.
I want to go home,
Please let me go home.
I feel so broke up,
I want to go home.

The first mate he got drunk,
He broke up the people's trunk.
The constable had to come and take him away.
Oh, Mr. John Stone,
Please let me go home.
I feel so broke up,
I want to go home.

So hoist up the John B sails,
See how the mainsail set.
Call for the captain ashore, let me go home.
I want to go home,
Please let me go home.
I feel so broke up,
I want to go home.

The first mate he got fits,
He ate all of me grits,
Then he come and he ate up all of me corn.
Oh, Mr. John Stone,
Please let me go home.
I feel so broke up,
I want to go home.

So hoist up the John B sails,
See how the mainsail set.
Call for the captain ashore, let me go home.
Let me go home,
I want to go home.
I feel so broke up,
I want to go home.

NOTES TO MY FELLOW "PICKERS"

As you review the lyrics to the songs printed on the following pages, you will see the chord names (with diagrams showing you where to put your fingers on the strings) above the words indicating where each new chord begins. I vary the lowest note (the bass note) on the chords you hear me playing on the CD. That choice of bass note is only indicated in a few places where I think it's really helpful to include it as a meaningful part of the character of the accompaniment of the song.

Finally, please don't feel you have to stick with the chords I'm playing at all. I'm always changing and developing my accompaniments—sometimes I change back to earlier chord patterns, then return again. In folk music, making these changes is not only allowed, it's expected and admired as part of a music that celebrates the gifts of each individual to interpret the music as he or she sees fit. Making changes to a folk song is called "the folk process," which means that new players change the song's lyrics, melody, rhythmic feel, and accompaniment to suit themselves and make the songs feel right and relevant in their own times.

Have fun creating your own folk process.
The songs will appreciate it and feel loved, I promise you.

The Golden Vanity

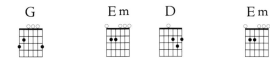

There was a ship that sailed all on the lowland sea,

And the name of the ship was the *Golden Vanity*.

And we feared she would be taken by the Spanish enemy

As she sailed upon the lowland, lowland, lowland,

Sailed upon the lowland sea.

Then up spoke the cabin boy, and boldly out spoke he,
And he said to our captain, "What will you give to me,
If I swim along the side of the Spanish enemy
And I sink her in the lowland, lowland, lowland,
Sink her in the lowland sea?"

"Oh, I will give you silver, and I will give you gold,
And my own fair young daughter, your bonny bright shall be,
If you'll swim along the side of the Spanish enemy
And you sink her in the lowland, lowland, lowland,
Sink her in the lowland sea.

Then the boy made him ready, and overboard sprang he,
And he swam along the side of the Spanish enemy.
With his brace and auger in her side he bored holes three,
And he sank her in the lowland, lowland, lowland,
Sank her in the lowland sea.

Then quickly he swam back to the cheering of the crew,
But the captain would not heed him, his promise he did rue.
And he scorned his poor entreatings when loudly he did sue,
And he left him in the lowland, lowland, lowland,
Left him in the lowland sea.

Then his messmates drew him up, but on the deck he died.
And they stitched him in a hammock which was so fair and white.
Then they lowered him overboard, and he drifted with the tide,
And he sank into the lowland, lowland, lowland,
Sank into the lowland sea.

There was a ship that sailed all on the lowland sea,
And the name of the ship was the *Golden Vanity*.
And we feared she would be taken by the Spanish enemy
As she sailed upon the lowland, lowland, lowland,
Sailed upon the lowland sea.

As she sailed upon the lowland, lowland, lowland,
Sailed upon the lowland sea.

Skip to My Lou

Chorus:

D

Skip, skip, skip to my Lou,

A

Skip, skip, skip to my Lou,

D

Skip, skip, skip to my Lou,

A   D

Skip to my Lou, my darlin'.

Lost my partner, what'll I do?
Lost my partner, what'll I do?
Lost my partner, what'll I do?
Skip to my Lou, my darlin'.

Chorus

I'll get another one, prettier than you,
I'll get another one, nicer than you,
I'll get another one, nicer than you,
Skip to my Lou, my darlin'.

Chorus

Fly's in the buttermilk, shoo, fly, shoo,
Fly's in the buttermilk, shoo, fly, shoo,
Fly's in the buttermilk, shoo, fly, shoo,
Skip to my Lou, my darlin'.

Chorus

Little red wagon painted blue,
Little red wagon painted blue,
Little red wagon painted blue,
Skip to my Lou, my darlin'.

Chorus

Cockles and Mussels

D   A

In Dublin's fair city, where girls are so pretty,

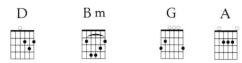
D   B m   G   A

There I first laid my eyes on sweet Molly Malone,

D

As she wheeled her wheelbarrow

A

Through the streets broad and narrow,

D   B m   G   A   D

Crying, "Cockles and mussels, alive, alive - o!"

Chorus:

D   A

"Alive, alive-o-oh! Alive, alive-o-oh!"

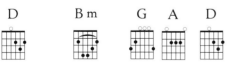
D   B m   G   A   D

Crying, "Cockles and mussels, alive, alive - o!"

She was a fishmonger, and sure 'twas no wonder,
'Cause her mother and father were fishmongers too.
And they all wheeled their barrow
Through the streets broad and narrow,
Crying, "Cockles and mussels, alive, alive-o!"

Chorus

She died of the fever, and no one could save her,
And that was the end of sweet Molly Malone.
Now her ghost wheels the barrow
Through the streets broad and narrow,
Crying, "Cockles and mussels, alive, alive-o!"

Chorus

The Fox

D

Oh, the fox went out on a chilly night,

A

Prayed for the moon to give him light,

D   G

For he had many a mile to go that night

D   A   D   A   D

Before he reached the town-o, town-o, town-o.

G   D   A   D

Many a mile to go that night before he reached the town-o.

He ran till he came to a great big pen
Where the ducks and the geese were kept therein.
He said, "A couple of you are gonna grease my chin
Before I leave this town-o, town-o, town-o.
A couple of you are gonna grease my chin
     before I leave this town-o!"

He grabbed the gray goose by the neck,
Flung him up across his back.
He didn't mind the "quack, quack, quack"
And the legs all danglin' down-o, down-o, down-o.
He didn't mind the "quack, quack, quack"
     and the legs all danglin' down-o.

Then old mother Flipper Flopper jumped out of bed,
Out of the window she popped her head,
Cryin', "John, John, the gray goose is gone
And the fox is on the town-o, town-o, town-o.
John! John! The gray goose is gone and
     the fox is on the town-o!"

Then John, he ran to the top of the hill,
Blew his horn both loud and shrill.
The fox, he said, "I better flee with my kill,
For they'll soon be on my trail-o, trail-o, trail-o."
The fox, he said, "I better flee with my kill,
     for they'll soon be on my trail-o!"

He ran till he came to his cozy den,
There were the little ones, eight, nine, ten.
They said, "Daddy, daddy, better go back again
'Cause it must be a mighty fine town-o, town-o, town-o.
Daddy, daddy, better go back again
     'cause it must be a mighty fine town-o!"

Then the fox and his wife, without any strife,
Cut up the goose with a carving knife.
They never had such a supper in their life,
And the little ones chewed on the
     bones-o, bones-o, bones-o.
They never had such a supper in their life,
     and the little ones chewed on the bones-o!

The fox went out on a chilly night,
Prayed for the moon to give him light,
He had many a mile to go that night
Before he reached the town-o, town-o, town-o.
Many a mile to go that night before
     he reached the town-o.

Springfield Mountain

E   B 7

On Springfield Mountain there did dwell

E

A lovely youth, I knowed him well-aye-el.

Chorus:

E   B 7

Too roody noo, too roody nay,

E

Too roody noo, too roody nay-aye-ay.

This lovely youth one day did go
Down to the meadow for to mow-aye-oh.

Chorus

He had not mowed quite round the field,
When a poison serpent bit his heel-aye-eel.

Chorus

They took him home to Molly dear,
Which made him feel so very queer-aye-eer.

Chorus

Now Molly had two ruby lips,
With which the poison she did sip-aye-ip.

Chorus

Now Molly had a rotten tooth,
And so the poison killed them booth-aye-ooth.

Chorus

On Springfield Mountain there did dwell
A lovely youth, I knowed him well-aye-el.

Chorus

The Erie Canal

Dm Dm/C   Gm   A

 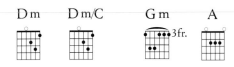

I've got a mule, her name is Sal,

Dm   A   Dm

Fifteen miles on the Erie Canal.

Dm   Dm/C   Gm   A

She's a good old worker and a good old pal,

Dm   A Dm

Fifteen miles on the Erie Canal.

F   C

We've loaded barges in our day

F   A

Filled with lumber, coal, and hay.

Dm   Dm/C Gm   A

And we know every   inch of the way

Dm   A Dm C

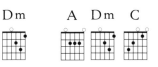

From Albany to Buffalo.

Chorus:

F   C7

Low bridge, everybody down!

F   C7 F

Low bridge, 'cause we're comin' into town!

F   B♭

And you'll always know your neighbor,

F   B♭

You'll always know your pal,

F   B♭   F C7 F A

If you've ever navigated the Erie Ca - nal.

We'd better look around for a job, old gal,
Fifteen miles on the Erie Canal.
'Cause you bet your life I'd never part with Sal,
Fifteen miles on the Erie Canal.

Get up there mule, here comes a lock.
We'll make Rome 'bout six o'clock.
And one more trip and back we'll go
Right back home to Buffalo.

Chorus

Beautiful City

If you place your capo on the 3rd fret and play in the key of A minor, this song will sound in the same key as on the CD: C minor.

Chorus:

A m (Cm)

O, what a beautiful city,

E (G)   A m (Cm)

O, what a beautiful city,

A m (Cm)

God knows, it's a beautiful city,

A m/G (Cm/B♭)   F (A♭)   Am   E   Am

Twelve gates to the city,   hallelu   -   jah.

A m (Cm)

Three gates to the north,

E (G)

Three gates to the south,

A m (Cm)

Three gates to the east,

E (G)

Three gates to the west.

A m/G (Cm/B♭)   F (A♭)   Am   E   Am

There's twelve gates to the city,   hallelu   -   jah.

Chorus

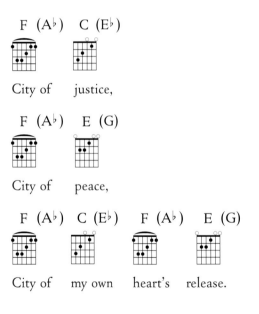

F (A♭)   C (E♭)

City of   justice,

F (A♭)   E (G)

City of   peace,

F (A♭)   C (E♭)   F (A♭)   E (G)

City of   my own   heart's   release.

Chorus

Rock-a My Soul

Chorus:

C

Rock my soul in the bosom of Abraham,

G

Rock my soul in the bosom of Abraham,

C

Rock my soul in the bosom of Abraham,

G   C

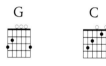

O, rock-a my soul!

C

So high I can't get over it,

G

So low I can't get under it,

C

So wide I can't get round it,

G   C

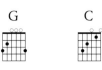

O, rock-a my soul!

C

Rock my soul,

G

Rock my soul,

C

Rock my soul,

G   C

Rock my soul.

Chorus

The Cruel War

If you place your capo on the 2nd fret and play in the key of C major,
this song will sound in the same key as on the CD: D major.

C (D) Am (Bm) Dm (Em) Em (F#m) E (F#)

The cruel war is raging, and Johnny has to fight.

F (G) Dm (Em) G (A) F (G) C (D)

I want to be with him from mor - ning till night.

C (D) Am (Bm) Dm (Em) Em (F#m)

I want to be with him, it grieves my heart so.

E (F#) F (G) Dm (Em)

Won't you let me go with you?

G (A) F (G) C (D)

No, my love, no.

Tomorrow is Sunday, and Monday is the day
That your captain will call you and you must obey.
Your captain will call you, it grieves my heart so.
Won't you let me go with you?
No, my love, no.

I'll tie back my hair, men's clothing I'll put on.
I'll pass as your comrade as we march along.
I'll pass as your comrade. No one will ever know.
Won't you let me go with you?
No, my love, no.

Your cheek is too ruddy, your fingers are too small,
Your skin still too fair to face the cannonball.
Won't you let me go with you? It grieves my heart so.
Won't you let me go with you?
No, my love, no.

Oh, Johnny, oh, Johnny, I fear you are unkind.
I love you far better than even my own life.
I love you far better than words can e'er express.
Won't you let me go with you?
Yes, my love, yes.

The cruel war is raging, and Johnny has to fight.
I want to be with him from morning till night.

O, Mary, Don't You Weep

Chorus:

E   B 7

O, Mary, don't you weep, don't you mourn,

                  E   E 7

O, Mary, don't you weep, don't you mourn.

A   E

Pharaoh's army got drownded,

    B 7   E

O, Mary, don't you weep.

If I could I surely would
Stand on the rock where Moses stood.
Pharaoh's army got drownded,
O, Mary, don't you weep.

Chorus

One of these mornings 'bout twelve o'clock,
This whole world's gonna reel and rock.
Pharaoh's army got drownded,
O, Mary, don't you weep.

Chorus

One of these mornings, and it won't be long,
We're gonna sing that freedom song.
Pharaoh's army got drownded,
O, Mary, don't you weep.

Chorus

I've Been Workin' on the Railroad

If you place your capo on the 4th fret and play in the key of C major,
this song will sound in the same key as on the CD: E major.

C (E)

I've been workin' on the railroad

F (A)   C (E)

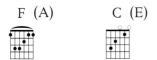

All the live long day.

C (E)

I've been workin' on the railroad

D7 (F♯7)   G7 (B7)

Just to pass the time away.

G (B)   C (E)

Can't ya hear the whistle blowing

F (A)   E7 (G♯7)

Rise up so early in the morn.

F (A)   C (E)

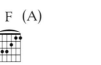

Can't you hear the captain shouting,

C (E)   G (B)   C (E)

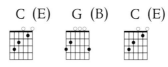

"Dinah,   blow your horn!"

C (E)

Dinah, won't you blow,

F (A)

Dinah, won't you blow,

G (B)   C (E)

Dinah, won't you blow your horn, your horn?

C (E)

Dinah, won't you blow,

F (A)

Dinah, won't you blow,

G (B) C (E)

Dinah, won't you blow your horn?

C (E)

Someone's in the kitchen with Dinah.

G (B)

Someone's in the kitchen, I know.

C (E) C7 (E7) F (A)

Someone's in the kitchen with Dinah,

C (E) G (B) C (E)

Strummin' on the old banjo, and singin'

C (E)

"Fee, fie, fiddle-y-i-o,

G (B)

Fee, fie, fiddle-y-i-o-o-o-o.

C (E) C7 (E7) F (A)

Fee, fie, fiddle-y-i-o."

G (B) C (E)

Strummin' on the old banjo.

Sloop John B

E

We sail on the sloop John B,

E

My grandfather and me.

B 7

'Round Nassau town we did go.

E   E 7

Drinking all night,

A   A m

Got into a fight.

E   B 7

I feel so broke up,

E

I want to go home.

Chorus:

So hoist up the John B sails,
See how the mainsail set.
Call for the captain ashore, let me go home.
I want to go home,
Please let me go home.
I feel so broke up,
I want to go home.

The first mate he got drunk,
He broke up the people's trunk.
The constable had to come and take him away.
Oh, Mr. John Stone,
Please let me go home.
I feel so broke up,
I want to go home.

Chorus

The first mate he got fits,
He ate all of me grits,
Then he come and he
    ate up all of me corn.
Oh, Mr. John Stone,
Please let me go home.
I feel so broke up,
I want to go home.

Chorus

About the Songs

The Golden Vanity

This old English ballad tells the story of a young sailor who tries to save his ship from the Spanish enemy. The captain promises him silver and gold, and his very own daughter, if the sailor will sink the enemy ship. This song was true-to-life because sailors not only experienced the dangers of long ocean voyages, but they sometimes faced cruel and heartless treatment by sea captains. The captain in this song may have been modeled after Sir Walter Raleigh who served in the court of Queen Elizabeth I.

Skip to My Lou

"Skip to My Lou" was the name of a popular game at parties on the American Frontier during the nineteenth century. With everyone in a circle, one boy would skip around the circle, choose a girl, link arms with her, and skip in a circle. That girl's former partner would skip after them and try to catch up to the couple before the girl made it back to her starting place. That's why the lyric says, "Lost my partner, what'll I do?"

Maybe you're wondering who Lou is? Lou was another word for "sweetheart." So Lou could be anybody you liked especially well!

Cockles and Mussels

It used to be that whatever job your parents did, you were pretty much expected to do that same job when you grew up. This song tells us that young Molly Malone was a fishmonger, a seller of fish in the city streets, just as her mother and father were before her. Today, young people are free to choose their profession. But not then! Some consider this song to be the unofficial people's anthem of Dublin, Ireland, but despite its Irish connection, it is believed to have been written by a man from Scotland many, many years ago.

The Fox

Foxes used to be a great menace to farms, so they were sometimes hunted to stop them from killing small farm animals like ducks and geese. But in this humorous song, we laugh at the farmers, John and Mrs. Flipper Flopper, and cheer for the fox instead. Folk songs like this one teach us that we can see the same story from many points of view and that a sense of humor about ourselves can help make scary events—like the one in this song—a lot less frightening, and just another part of life.

Springfield Mountain

This song is based on the story of Timothy Myrick's fatal snakebite in Connecticut in 1761. Though the subject is serious, you have to laugh at the story's conclusion and enjoy the silly way the lyrics are pronounced; "well" becomes "well-ay-el" and "mow" becomes "mow-aye-oh." It may be that this song was intended to warn children about snakes, but there's no doubt that the fun of singing it is what has made the song last more than two hundred years.

The Erie Canal

The Erie Canal, finished in 1825, connected Lake Erie to the Hudson River. Stretching 363 miles, it was an engineering wonder and at the time the longest canal in America or Europe. Mules like Sal walked along the side of the canal pulling the floating barges filled with produce or other goods. The canal became so popular that it was enlarged several times till finally it stretched (as the song says) all the way "from Albany to Buffalo." This song, one that helped to build America, is so filled with fun images of those exciting times that you feel as though you are almost there on the barge hauled by good old Sal.

Beautiful City

This African-American spiritual refers to a city described in the New Testament of the Bible: a promised city that sparkles like a gem, with walls 1,400 miles long, wide, and high. Originally sung by African-American slaves, this song speaks of peace and justice in heaven. "Beautiful City" also provided a secret way for slaves to tell each other that they yearned for freedom in their own lifetimes, not just in heaven. We know that slaves could not have openly sung these thoughts, or their slave masters would have punished them severely.

Rock-a My Soul

This spiritual is one of the best and most joyous songs for multipart singing by a trio, or for division into audience parts, which is the way I recorded it on a Peter, Paul, & Mary album. In this song's biblical story, a poor beggar named Lazarus is scorned in his lifetime, but when he dies, the angels honor him by bringing him to Abraham. Abraham rocks Lazarus lovingly, like a baby, reminding us that both the wealthiest and the poorest of people who have good and caring hearts are worthy of great love and honor.

The Cruel War

This song can be traced back to the Civil War, but it almost certainly came from a much earlier version written in England. We pity this girl who loves Johnny so much that she begs him to let her accompany him to battle. We know that Johnny does not want to leave her behind, but he also wants to protect her from the terrible dangers she would face if she came with him. In the end, what matters to both characters is that they are together and safe in their love, regardless of the perils that surround them.

O, Mary, Don't You Weep

This song tells of the triumph of the Jewish people who were delivered from slavery under Pharaoh, the ruler of Egypt in biblical times. African-American spirituals often refer to this history because both Jews and African-Americans were once slaves. As with other spirituals, this song helps to unite people in the cause of freedom. "O, Mary" recalls the history of those who have suffered great injustice—and also reminds us that it is our responsibility to make sure that, one day, all people who are enslaved or deprived of their rights must be freed from such oppression.

I've Been Workin' on the Railroad

What does someone playing a banjo in Dinah's kitchen have to do with the railroad? This song is fascinating to me because, although the sections don't seem connected at all, they work well together. Initially published in 1894, the song was first recorded in 1927 by the Sandheels Sixteen. Some say the song came from African-American workers in Louisiana who were building the river levees. Others think it originated with Irish immigrant workers who made their way out west during the construction of the American railroad. Maybe, like many folk songs, it traveled, and both are partially true.

Sloop John B

This folk song comes from the Bahaman Islands in the West Indies. It expresses a feeling we all have when real life turns out to be less wonderful than we had hoped it might be. This song, which tells of a hard time at sea, moves us and reminds us that we all yearn to be in a place where we are appreciated, welcomed, and cared about. You can hear the longing in this song's words and melodies, and when I sing it, I imagine a world of greater peace and justice. Singing "Sloop John B" helps to remind us what is really important in life.

About the Author

Peter Yarrow's career has spanned close to five decades as a member of the legendary folk trio Peter, Paul, & Mary, who became known to many as a voice of their generation's conscience, awakening and inspiring others to help make the world a more just, equitable, and peaceful place. Today, Yarrow devotes the majority of his time to running Operation Respect, a nonprofit he founded in 1999 that received a unanimous vote of Congress honoring its work to create respectful, safe, and bully-free environments for children in schools across America and beyond. Besides numerous awards for his artistry and his public service, Peter has received two honorary doctorates for his steadfast work in the educational arena.

For many years, Peter Yarrow dreamed of recording his favorite folk songs in a very simple, intimate way—the way he first heard them sung as a child. Along with his daughter, Bethany Yarrow, a gifted singer in her own right, Peter shares the songs that first moved and inspired him to become the renowned folk singer he is today. When asked what he would most want to give the generations that follow him, Peter said, "I would give them these songs that helped me come to realize what, for me, is really important in life—people, love, work, and service to each other. I believe that all children can be helped to discover what's important to them in their lives, through these songs. It's magic, in a way, but it seems to happen every time!"

About the Illustrator

Terry Widener's relationship with folk music began as a child in Oklahoma, where he was surrounded by classic folk songs performed by singers like Woody Guthrie. Folk music had made a big impact on the region during the Dustbowl era, and as Terry grew up, this music was an essential part of his heritage.

Inspired by a passion for art, Terry studied graphic design at the University of Tulsa. He has illustrated more than twenty books, including *If the Shoe Fits* by Gary Soto, *Steel Town* by Jonah Winter, and *Lou Gehrig: The Luckiest Man* by David Adler. His picture books have won numerous accolades including a Boston Globe–Horn Book Honor Award, an ALA Notable Children's Book Award, and the California Young Reader Medal.

A father of three, Terry currently resides in McKinney, Texas, with his wife, Leslie.

CD Credits

Produced by Peter Yarrow

Peter Yarrow: Lead Vocals, Guitar

Bethany Yarrow: Lead Vocals

Paul Prestopino: Banjo, Mandolin, Mandola, Guitars
 (6 string and 12 string), Dobro, Ukulele, Harmonica

Rufus Cappadocia: Cello on "Beautiful City"

Recorded at Midwood Studios, Brooklyn, New York

Recording Engineer: Glen Marshall

First Mix Engineers: Glen Marshall, Tom Swift

Final Mix Engineer: Kevin Salem, Woodstock, New York

Mastering Conversion & Mastering Prep: Kevin Salem,
 Woodstock, New York

Mastering: Howie Weinberg, Masterdisk, New York, New York

PY Productions Staff: Beth Bradford, Rachel Jackson, Tony Arancio

Musical transcriptions by Robert Agis

Special Thanks

Paula Allen, Tony Arancio, Beth Bradford, Che and Zachary Cappadocia, Louise Daniels, Kaylee Davis, Meaghan Finnerty, Frances Gilbert, Sebastian Gross-Ossa, Rachel Jackson, Marcus Leaver, Bill Luckey, Charlie Nurnberg, Valentina Ossa, Lisa Palattella, Scott Piehl, Mary Rower, Jacquie Turner, Mary Beth Yarrow